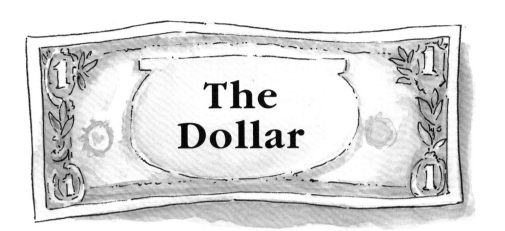

The Dollar

by Nathan Zimelman
illustrated by Deborah Zemke

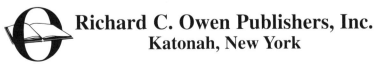
Richard C. Owen Publishers, Inc.
Katonah, New York

Archie Jones found a dollar
on the sidewalk one day.

He wanted to share his good luck
and buy presents for his friends.

One friend said,
"I'd like a comic book, please."

One friend said,
"I'd like a race car, please."

One friend said,
"I'd like baseball cards, please."

All of that cost more than one dollar.

Archie walked down the street to think.
He passed Mr. Greene's candy store.

He saw a huge jar of jelly beans in the window.
Archie opened the door and went in.

"I would like one dollar's worth
of jelly beans, if you please," said Archie.

Mr. Greene popped open a striped paper bag.
"I will scoop up one dollar's worth
of jelly beans for you," he said.
"Thank you," said Archie.

Archie walked up the street
and gave jelly beans to all his friends.

When he was done,
there were ten jelly beans
left in the striped paper bag.

"For me!" said Archie.
And he ate the ten jelly beans.